**For Swee Hong
and James**

*There are days when Bartholomew is naughty,
and other days when he is very very good.*

First published 1991 by Walker Books Ltd, 87 Vauxhall Walk, London SE11 5HJ

© 1991 Virginia Miller

First printed 1991
Printed and bound in Hong Kong by South China Printing Co. (1988) Ltd

British Library Cataloguing in Publication Data
Miller, Virginia
On your potty.
I. Title
823'.914 [J]

ISBN 0-7445-1925-X

ON YOUR POTTY!

Virginia Miller

WALKER BOOKS
LONDON

One morning George padded quietly over to
Bartholomew's bed to see if he was awake.
He asked softly, "Are you awake, Ba?"

"Nah!" said Bartholomew.

George asked, "Are you up, Ba?"

"Nah!" said Bartholomew.

George asked,

"Do you need your potty, Ba?"

"Nah!" said Bartholomew.

"Nah,   nah,

nah, nah, NAH!" said Bartholomew.

"On your

potty!"

George said
in a big voice.

Bartholomew

sat on his potty.

He tried …

and he tried ...   **but nothing happened.**

"Nah!" said Bartholomew
in a little voice.

"Never mind," said George.

"Out you go and play, and be good."

"Nah!" said Bartholomew,

and off he went.

Suddenly Bartholomew thought,

On your potty!

He ran …

and he ran ...

as fast as he could …

and reached his potty …

just … in … time.

He padded proudly off to find George,

who gave him a great big hug.

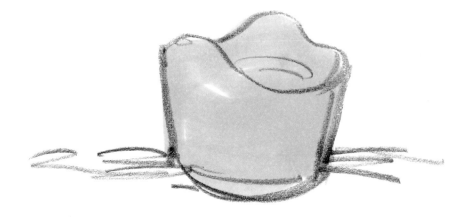